Eva for President

VOTE

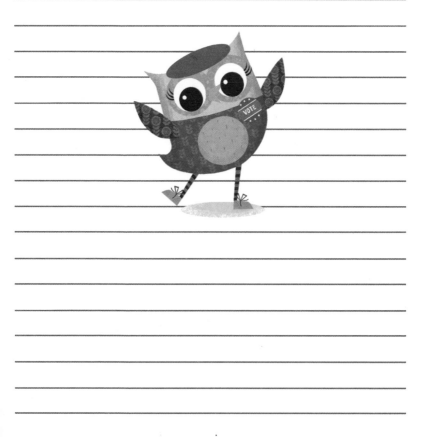

Read more
OWL DIARIES books!

1. Eva's Treetop Festival
2. Eva Sees a Ghost
3. A Woodland Wedding
4. Eva and the New Owl
5. Warm Hearts Day

6. Buster Is Missing
7. The Wildwood Bakery
8. Eva and the Lost Pony
9. Eva's Big Sleepover
10. Eva and Baby Mo

11. Trip to the Pumpkin Farm
12. Eva's Campfire Adventure
13. Eva in the Spotlight
14. Eva at the Beach
15. Eva's New Pet

16. Get Well, Eva
17. Eva in the Band
18. The Nature Club
19. Eva For President
20. The Owlympic Games

OWL DIARIES

♡ Eva for President ♡

Rebecca Elliott

BRANCHES

SCHOLASTIC INC.

For the lovely Charlie. Although heaven
help us if he is ever in charge. X — R.E.

Special thanks to Erica J. Chen for
her contributions to this book.

Copyright © 2024 by Rebecca Elliott

All rights reserved. Published by Scholastic Inc., *Publishers
since 1920.* SCHOLASTIC, BRANCHES, and associated logos are
trademarks and/or registered trademarks of Scholastic Inc.

The publisher does not have any control over and does not assume any
responsibility for author or third-party websites or their content.

No part of this publication may be reproduced, stored in a retrieval system, or transmitted
in any form or by any means, electronic, mechanical, photocopying, recording, or otherwise,
without written permission of the publisher. For information regarding permission, write to
Scholastic Inc., Attention: Permissions Department, 557 Broadway, New York, NY 10012.

This book is a work of fiction. Names, characters, places, and incidents are either the
product of the author's imagination or are used fictitiously, and any resemblance to actual
persons, living or dead, business establishments, events, or locales is entirely coincidental.

Library of Congress Cataloging-in-Publication Data
Names: Elliott, Rebecca, author, illustrator.
Title: Eva for president / Rebecca Elliott.
Description: First edition. | New York : Branches/Scholastic, Inc. 2024. |
Series: Owl diaries ; 19 | Audience: Ages 5-7. | Audience: Grades K-2 |
Summary: Eva and Sue run for class president.
Identifiers: LCCN 2023019547 (print) | LCCN 2023019548 (ebook) | ISBN 9781338880274
(paperback) | ISBN 9781338880281 (library binding) |
ISBN 9781338880298 (ebook)
Subjects: CYAC: Owls–Fiction. | Elections–Fiction. | Schools–Fiction. |
BISAC: JUVENILE FICTION / Readers / Chapter Books | JUVENILE FICTION /
Animals / Birds | LCGFT: Animal fiction.
Classification: LCC PZ7.E45812 Epl 2024 (print) | LCC PZ7.E45812 (ebook)
| DDC [Fic]–dc23
LC record available at https://lccn.loc.gov/2023019547

ISBN 978-1-338-88028-1 (hardcover) / ISBN 978-1-338-88027-4 (paperback)

10 9 8 7 6 5 4 3 2 1   24 25 26 27 28

Printed in India   197
First edition, January 2024

Edited by Cindy Kim
Book design by Marissa Asuncion

♡ Table of Contents ♡

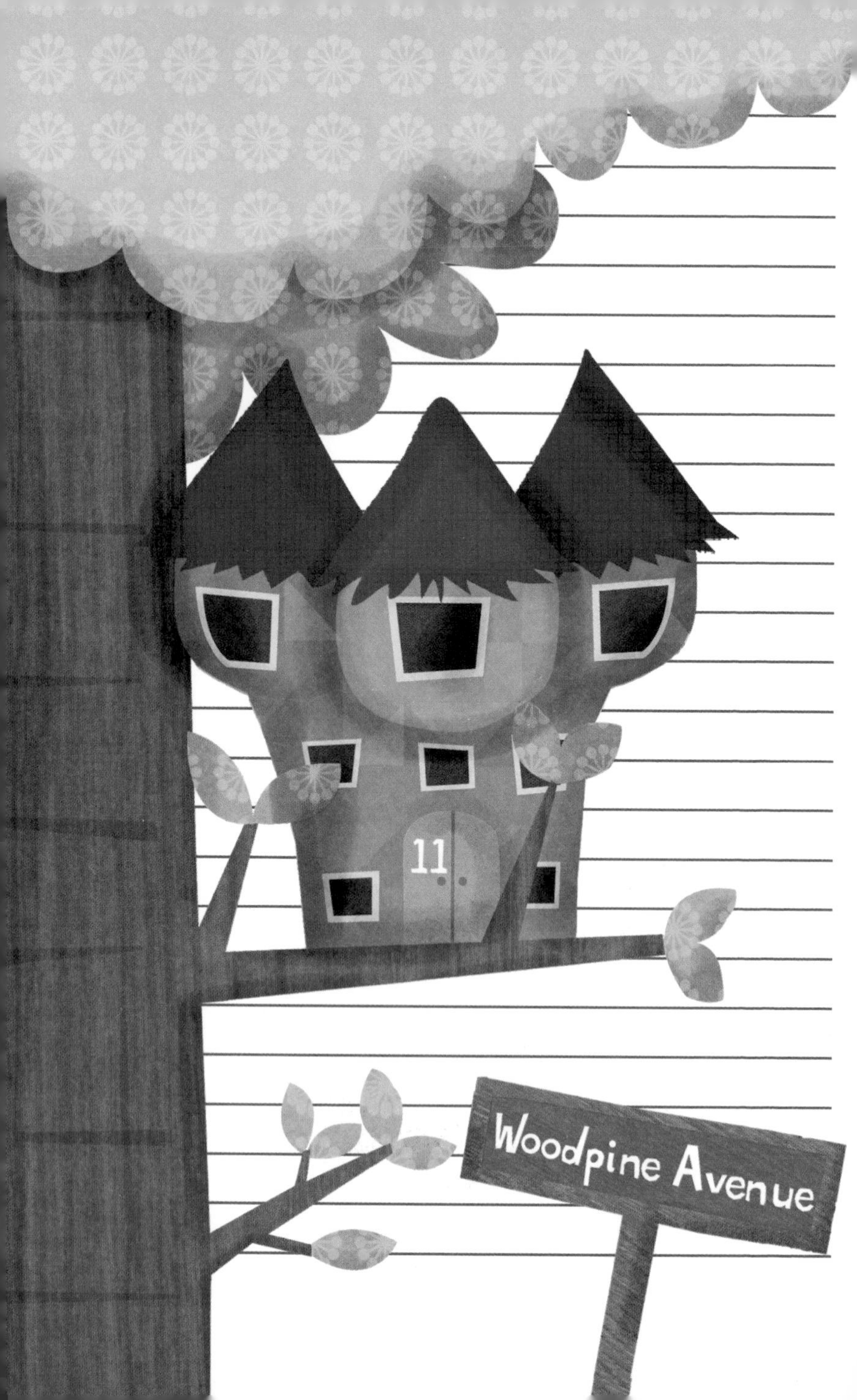
11
Woodpine Avenue

♡ Election Time ♡

Sunday

Hello, lovely Diary!
   It's me again, Eva the owl!

   I'm super excited because this week
we will be choosing our class president! I
wonder who it will be?!

I love:

Flags – this is
the United Owls
of the World flag!

Making posters

Making choices

Storytime

Helping
Mrs. Featherbottom

Ringing Barry
the Bell

Bing-a-ling-a-ling!

Doing fun
homework

The word <u>happy</u>

I DO NOT love:

Trying to fly a
flag when there
is no wind

Making mistakes

Waiting in
long lines

Cleaning up

NOT being picked to be Mrs. Featherbottom's helper

NOT getting to ring Barry the Bell

Doing boring homework

The word <u>sad</u>

I love my family! Here we are sharing a big Wingdale hug.

Mom

Dad

Me   Baby Mo   Humphrey

And these are my **WING-CREDIBLY** cute pets – Baxter the bat and Acorn the flying squirrel. They give great hugs, too!

Being an owl is the BEST.

We can quietly fly really fast.

We are **NOCTURNAL**, which means we stay awake at night, and go to sleep during the day.

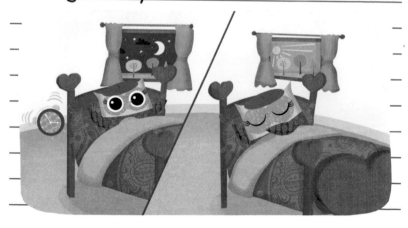

We have very long legs hidden under our feathers.

We also have super-hearing!

I live in a blue tree house on Woodpine Avenue in the town of Treetopolis. My **BFF** (best feathery friend), Lucy, lives in the orange tree house next door.

I go to Treetop Owlementary with lots of other friends. Here is my class and our teacher:

Sue

George   Zara   Zac

Kiera   Hailey

Carlos

Mrs.   Lucy   Me   Macy   Jacob   Lilly

Featherbottom

I can't wait to go to school tomorrow and find out more about this class president thing!

2

♡ HOO's Running? ♡

Monday

    At school this evening, Mrs. Featherbottom asked us what we wanted to be when we grow up.

As everyone started to share, I could feel my cheeks turn red.

But that was just it — I liked doing too many things!

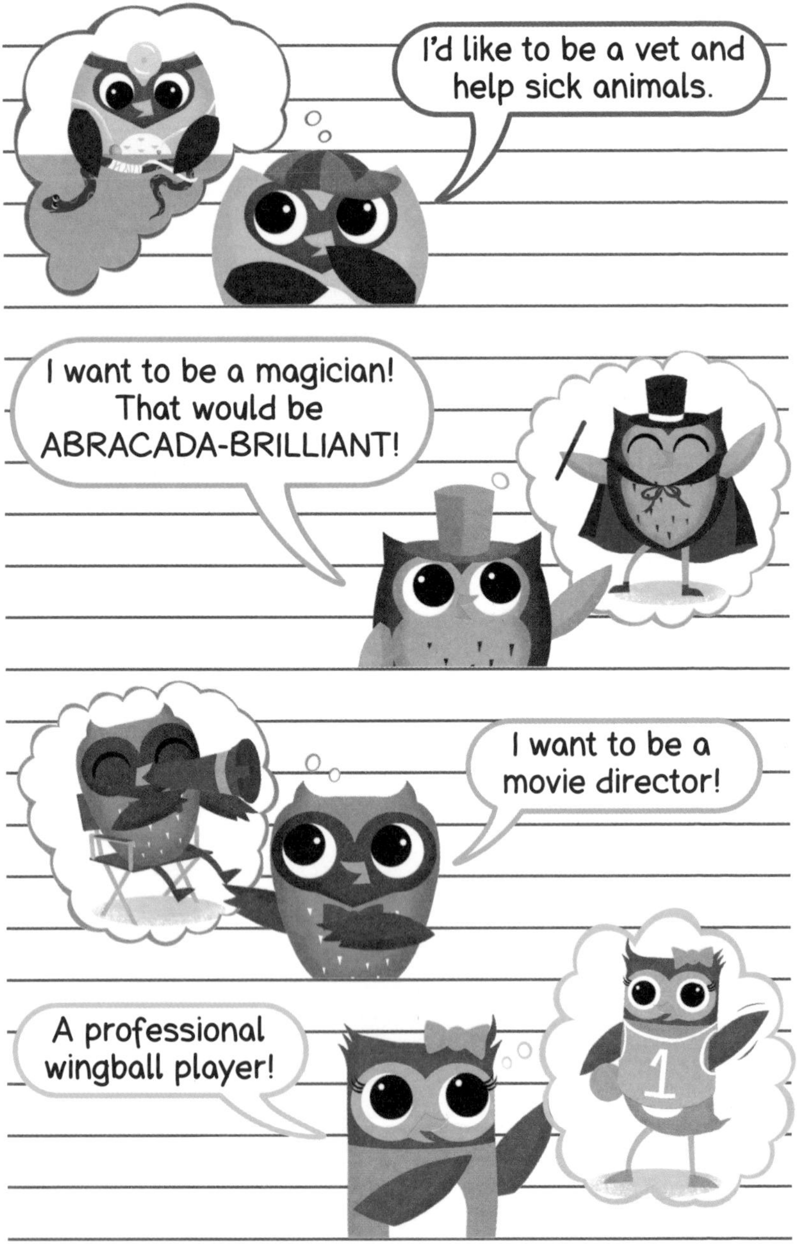
I'd like to be a vet and help sick animals.
I want to be a magician! That would be ABRACADA-BRILLIANT!
I want to be a movie director!
A professional wingball player!
1

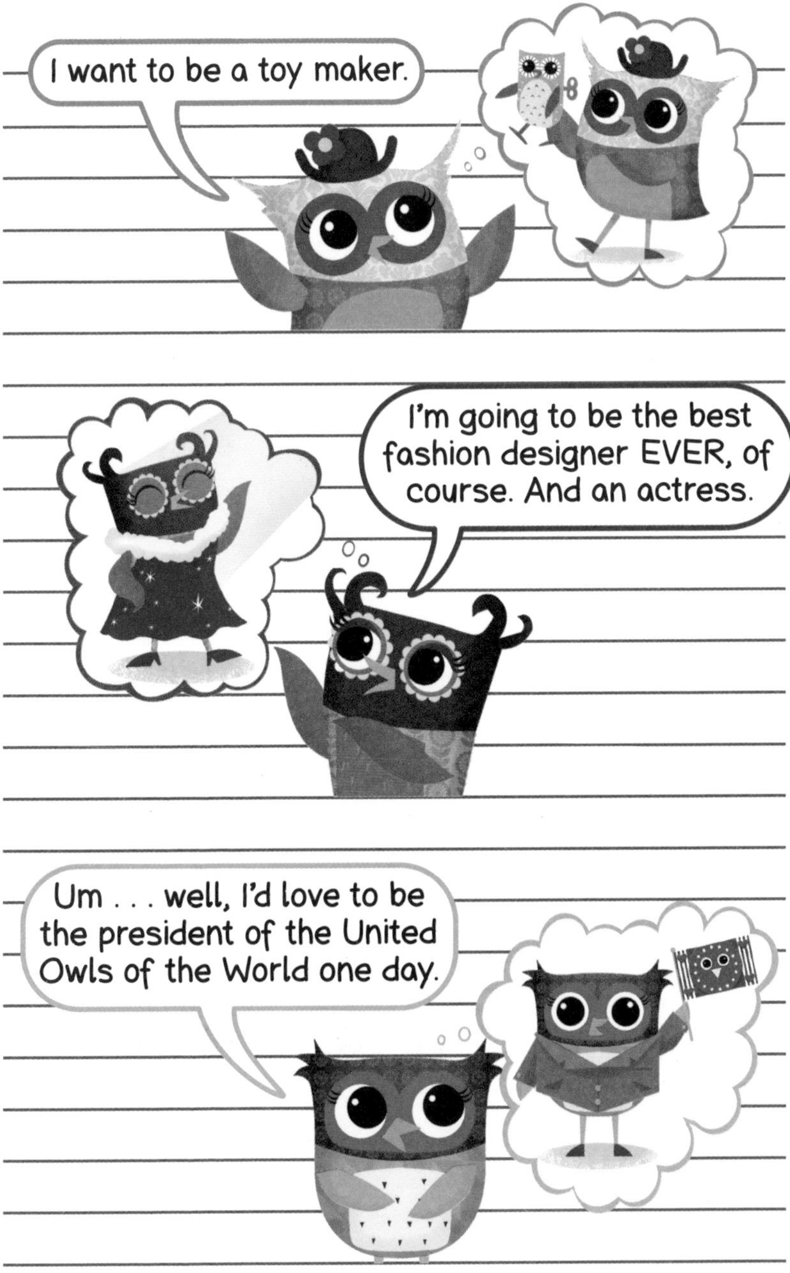
I want to be a toy maker.
I'm going to be the best fashion designer EVER, of course. And an actress.
Um . . . well, I'd love to be the president of the United Owls of the World one day.

My ears perked up. Hailey had a really big and really cool dream.

Then Mrs. Featherbottom turned to me.

So many ideas raced through my head!

After everyone shared their ideas,
Mrs. Featherbottom waved her wing.

As you all know, we will be choosing a class president this Friday. Please let me know who wants to run for election by the end of today.

Running? If it's a running race, I'll definitely win!

No, you won't, George — I'm faster than you!

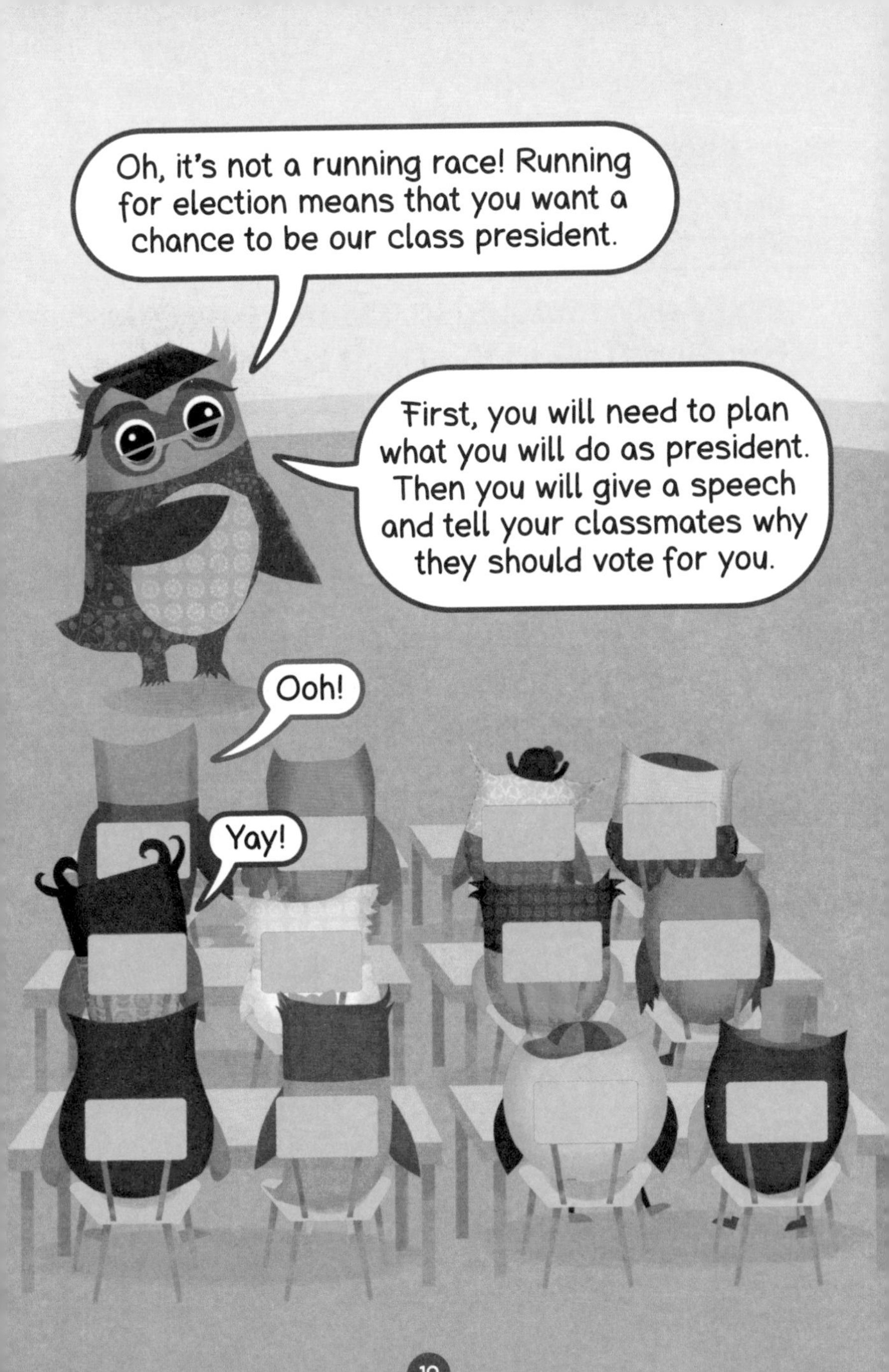
Oh, it's not a running race! Running for election means that you want a chance to be our class president.
First, you will need to plan what you will do as president. Then you will give a speech and tell your classmates why they should vote for you.
Ooh!
Yay!

I sort of liked the idea of being class president. Then I bet I could help Mrs. Featherbottom in our classroom every day. I wanted to ask more questions. But Sue flew to the front of the room.

Yes, Sue?

I definitely want to run for class president!

Very good, Sue! Who else wants to run? Let me know after recess.

At lunchtime, Sue stayed behind to make a plan on how to win everyone's vote. The rest of us went to lunch as usual.

So, is anyone else thinking of running?

I don't think there's any point. If Sue is running, she'll definitely win!

That's true. I would be nervous to run against Sue!

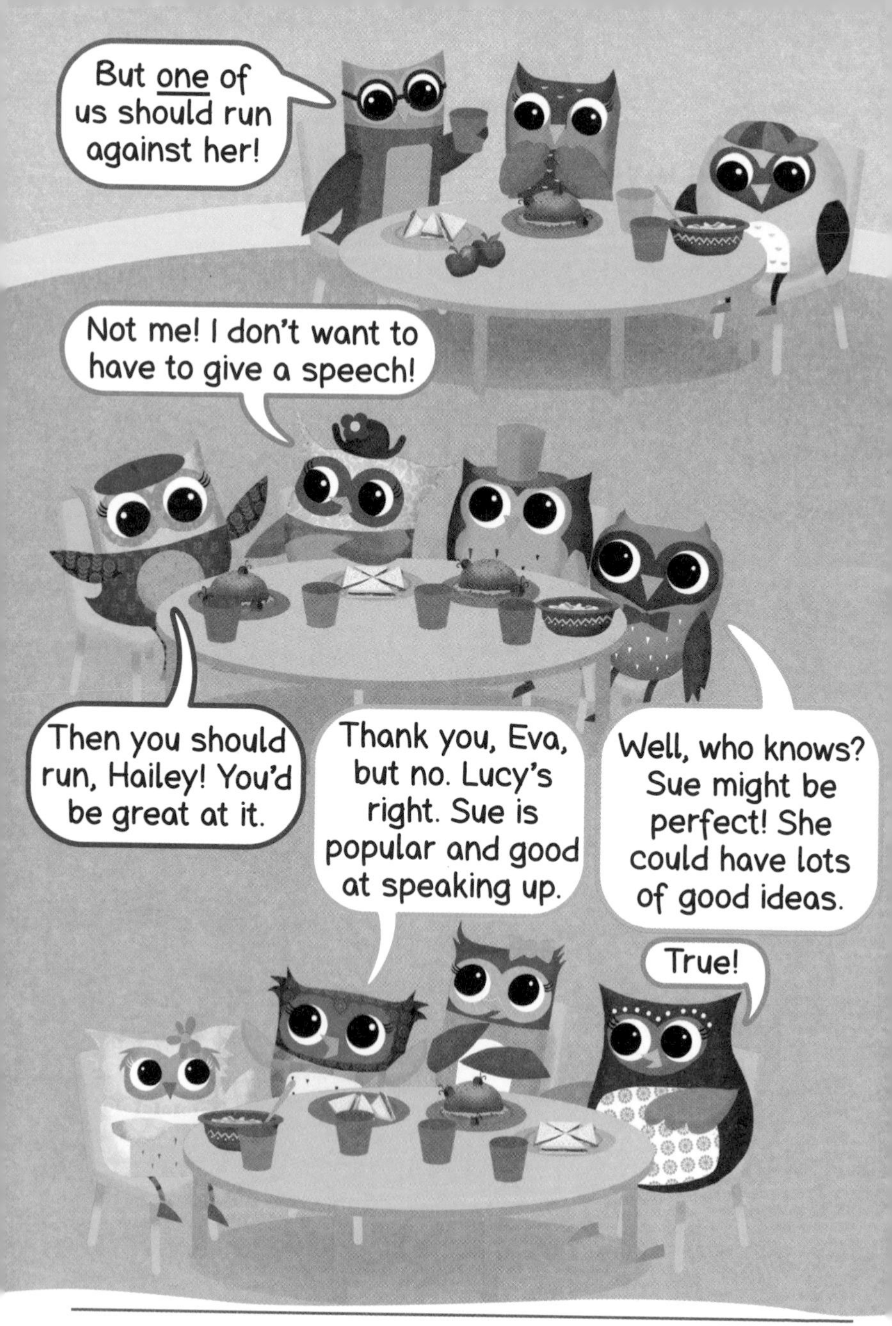
But one of us should run against her!
Not me! I don't want to have to give a speech!
Then you should run, Hailey! You'd be great at it.
Thank you, Eva, but no. Lucy's right. Sue is popular and good at speaking up.
Well, who knows? Sue might be perfect! She could have lots of good ideas.
True!

So like everyone else, I decided not to run. I didn't like the idea of having to try to beat Sue! But I was sad that no one else was running because that means we won't get to vote.

At the end of the day, our teacher made another announcement.

That's when I did a silly thing, Diary.
Before I knew it, I threw my wing in the air.

Everyone stared at me. And Sue's stare didn't look friendly.

THIS WEEK'S SCHEDULE

Tuesday (tomorrow) –
Eva and Sue make a plan

1. ═══
2. ═══
3. ═══

Wednesday – Speech Day!

Thursday – Class Debate & VOTING

✓

VOTE!

Friday – Tally up the results!

☐ SUE ☑ SUE
☑ EVA ☐ EVA

Oh, Diary. What have I done? This week could end in a DISASTER!

♡ If I Was in Charge ♡

Tuesday

I didn't sleep very well last night because I was busy worrying about what I had signed up for. But I woke up with a great idea!

I should ask Lucy and Hailey to help me!

As we flew to school, I asked them about it.

When we got to class, Sue told me that Zara was helping her run for president.

Then Sue turned to Jacob.

Jacob, you can be my other helper.

Me? Sure. Happy to help!

Later in the day, Mrs. Featherbottom gave Sue's team and my team some time to plan what we'd do as class president.

I looked down at my blank paper and ruffled my feathers.

Wow, Diary. Hailey really is very good at this stuff!

So we spent the rest of the day asking our classmates questions.

Our two big questions were:

Afterward, we looked through all the answers.

Well, the good news is some of this stuff is super helpful.

And some of the answers are just funny ones.

Lilly thinks school would be better if we were taught by unicorns.

Well, that is true!

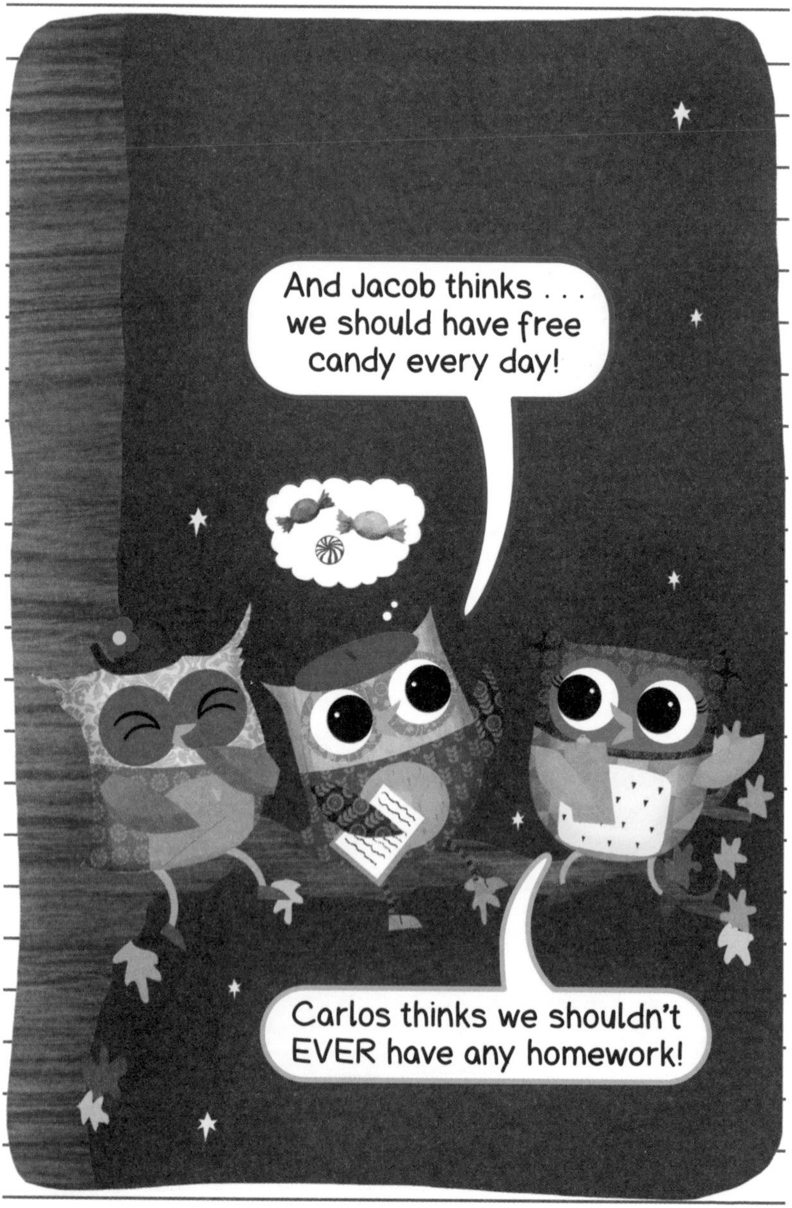
And Jacob thinks . . . we should have free candy every day!
Carlos thinks we shouldn't EVER have any homework!

Hailey, Lucy, and I agreed these were fun ideas, but not really things that would make school better for us.

Zac would love it if there were more books to read at school.
Macy wants more school clubs she can join.
And Zara wished that homework could be easier.
These are great ideas. So what do we do with them?

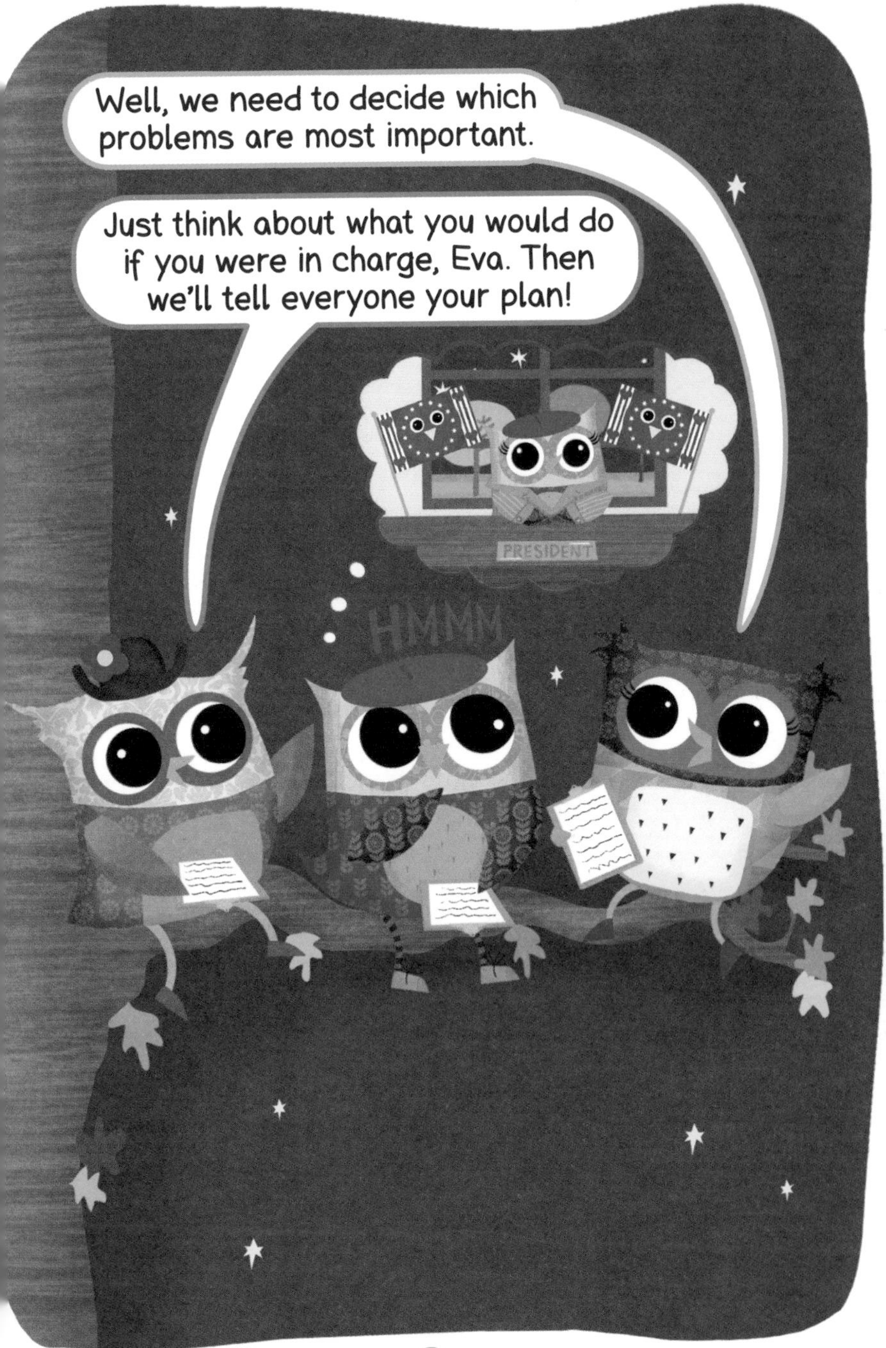
Well, we need to decide which problems are most important.
Just think about what you would do if you were in charge, Eva. Then we'll tell everyone your plan!
PRESIDENT
HMMM

TO-DO LIST

- Come up with a slogan

- Make a plan of everything I want to do as president

- Make badges and posters

- Practice answering questions for the debate

Oh dear Diary, at bedtime there were too many ideas floating around in my head. But I did think of a good slogan — I can't wait to tell Lucy and Hailey tomorrow!

♡ I'm Never Going to Win ♡

Wednesday

The next morning at school, Hailey, Lucy, and I held an important meeting.

Lucy had made cool badges for us.

> Wow! These are amazing, Lucy! You're so talented!
>
> Thank you, Eva!

I took a deep breath. Then I told them my idea for a slogan.

I was so pleased they liked my slogan! Now I had to tell them the bad news . . .

I hadn't thought up any good things I could do as president.

Oh, don't worry, Eva. I've been thinking about it, too. And I came up with ideas.

Wow, Hailey! These are brilliant! You are SO good at this!

Thank you, Eva! And you're so good at encouraging people!

After recess, Mrs. Featherbottom told me and Sue it was time to give the class our speeches. I pulled out Hailey's notes.

I was SUPER nervous. My feathers were shaking.

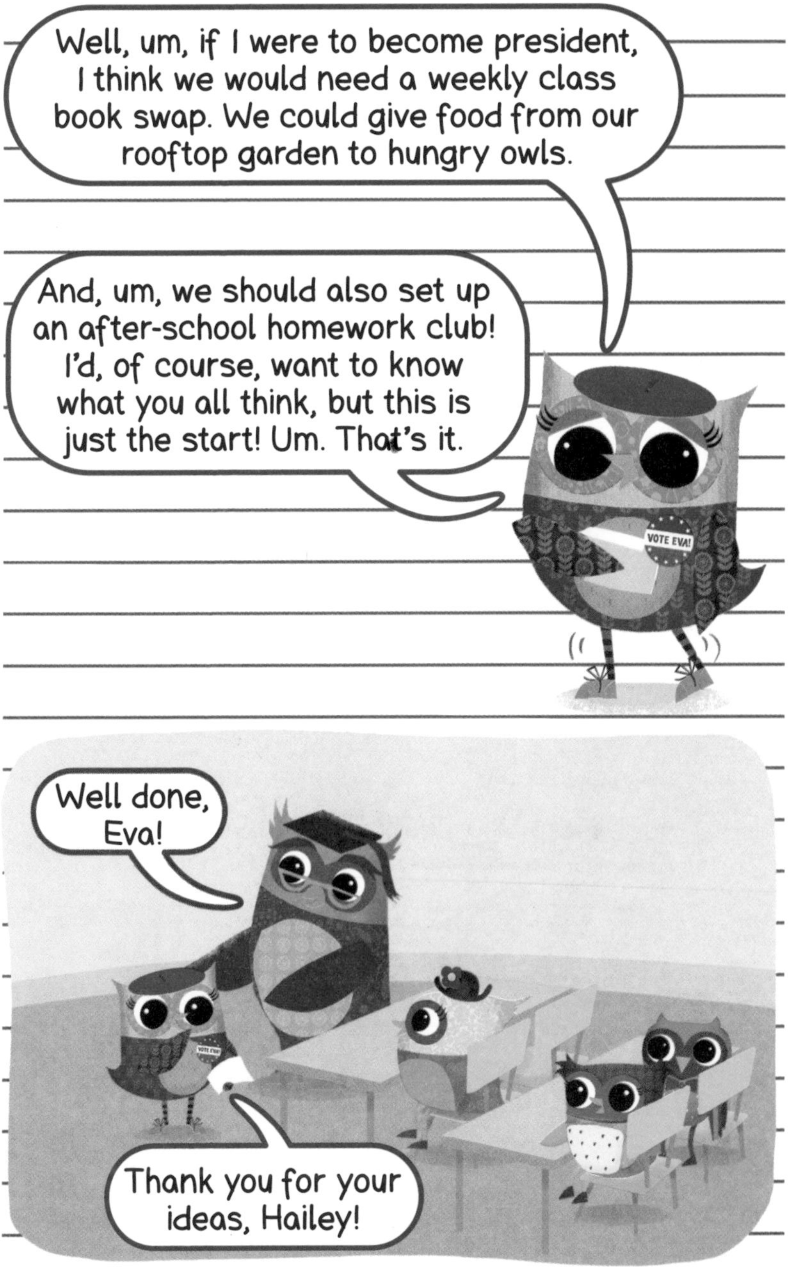
Well, um, if I were to become president, I think we would need a weekly class book swap. We could give food from our rooftop garden to hungry owls.
And, um, we should also set up an after-school homework club! I'd, of course, want to know what you all think, but this is just the start! Um. That's it.
VOTE EVA!
Well done, Eva!
Thank you for your ideas, Hailey!

As I nervously walked back to my seat, Sue danced up to the front, giving out candy to the class as she went.

Then she did a backflip and gave out more candy. The class clapped their wings and cheered.

I knew right away that there was no way I was going to win this election.

Um, okay! Well, everyone, back to work. The debate between Sue and Eva will happen tomorrow!

Mrs. Featherbottom reminded us that we need to really know our ideas well before the debate on Thursday.

After school, Lucy and Hailey came over to help me practice for the debate.

I did terribly today. And Sue was so good!

No, you weren't terrible! Don't worry, Eva. You just need to get your message out!

And I'm sure the rest of the class will realize that Sue's ideas are too wild!

Okay. So how does a debate work?

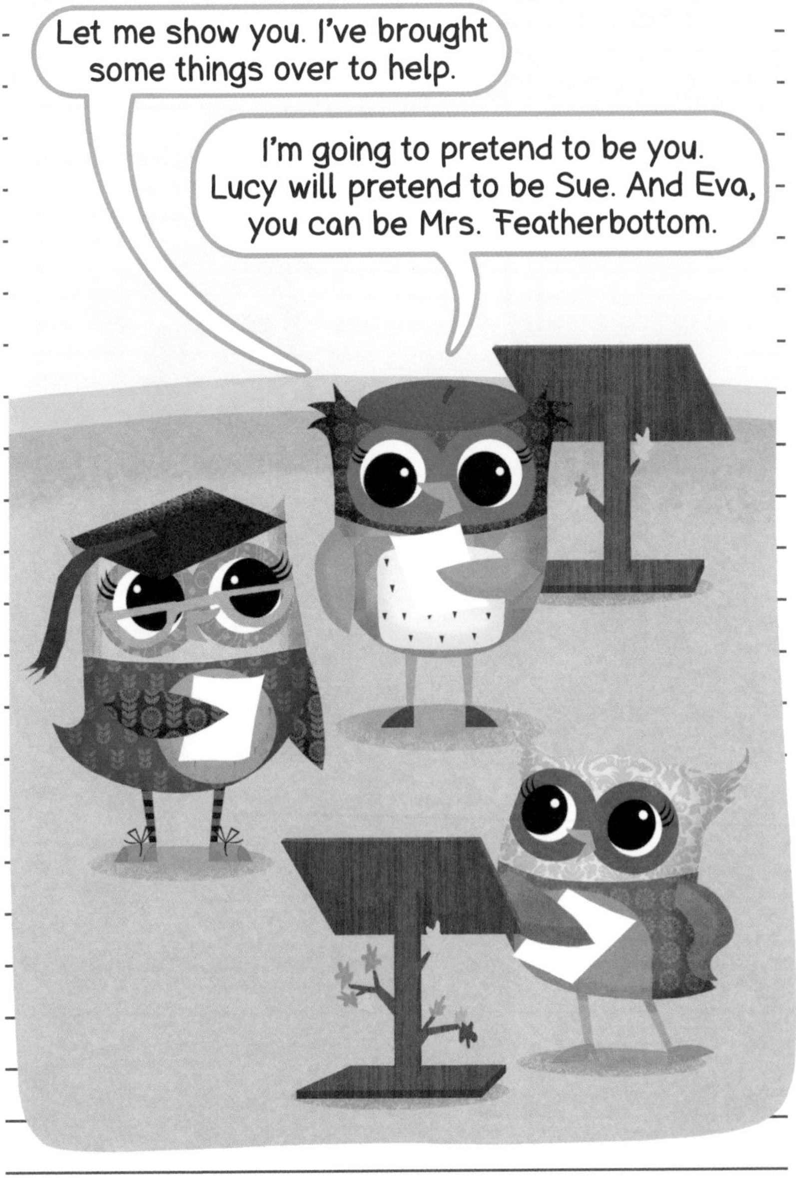
Let me show you. I've brought some things over to help.
I'm going to pretend to be you. Lucy will pretend to be Sue. And Eva, you can be Mrs. Featherbottom.

We had so much fun pretending to be different people! The more we practiced, the better I felt about answering questions.

After Hailey flew home for dinner, I chatted with Lucy.

Hailey is SO good at all this stuff!

Well, she does want to be the actual president when she grows up.

Oh, that's right! I'd totally forgotten about that!

I couldn't believe that in all the election madness I had forgotten what Hailey had said in class on Monday! After Lucy flew home, I had the perfect idea that would help us win! But it means I'll need to stay up VERY late tonight, Diary!!

♡ The New Plan ♡

Thursday

Before school, I met with Hailey and Lucy.

How are you feeling about the debate today, Eva?

Not good. There's a problem with our plan.

Oh no? What?

The wrong owl is running for president!

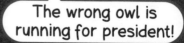

Then I took out the new posters I had made last night.

Hailey, I'm not very good at this president thing, but you REALLY are. And you've got what it takes to be the actual president one day! So why not start now?

At first, Hailey wasn't sure.

Are you sure you don't want to be president, Eva? And do you really think I can beat Sue?

I'm SO sure. And whether you win or not, it doesn't matter. What matters is that you get up there and go after your dreams!

You can do this, Hailey. And me and Eva are right behind you.
The three of us make a GREAT team.
Yes, we really do! Okay I'll do it. Thank you, Eva.
HOO CARES ABOUT OUR SCHOOL?
HAILEY THAT'S HOO!

At school, we put up the new posters and Lucy quickly made some new "Vote Hailey" badges and handed them out.

I told Mrs. Featherbottom that Hailey was now running in my place.

The truth is I don't think I want to be class president. But I know Hailey would be great at it!

That's a really honest decision, Eva. And thank you for stepping in, Hailey!

Later this afternoon, Sue and Hailey will have a debate. Then after that you will all make your vote for who you want to be class president!

During recess, Lucy helped Hailey prepare for the debate while I helped Mrs. Featherbottom set up the classroom.

I was allowed to ring Barry the Bell at the end of recess!

When the class came back inside, Hailey looked excited. I would have been so nervous! I was glad Hailey was running, and not me.

Good luck, Hailey! You got this!

Thanks, Eva!

The debate went great. We all asked Hailey and Sue questions. They both spoke really well. And they were kind to each other, even when they disagreed.

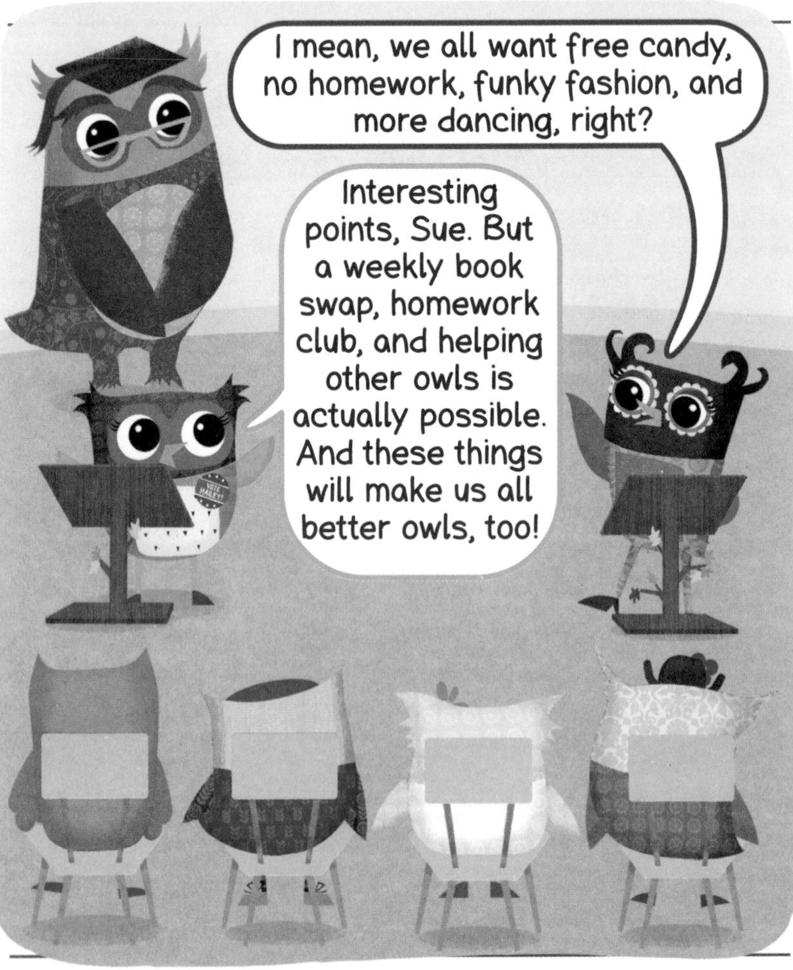
I mean, we all want free candy, no homework, funky fashion, and more dancing, right?
Interesting points, Sue. But a weekly book swap, homework club, and helping other owls is actually possible. And these things will make us all better owls, too!
VOTE HAILEY!

After a thoughtful debate, it was finally time to vote.

Well, Diary, maybe I still don't know what I want to be when I grow up. But at least I know I <u>don't</u> want to be president!

Tomorrow is results day. I wonder who will win!

♡ The New President ♡

In school the next morning, we all sat nervously waiting for Mrs. Featherbottom to share the election news.

We all clapped and cheered – even Sue!

Then Hailey gave a speech.

Then Hailey looked over at Sue with a big smile.

Sue, I was wondering . . . Would you like to be my vice president? As vice president, we would work together to help the class.

Of course, Hailey! I'll be the most stylish VP of all time!

Great! So I think my first job as president will be to make one of Sue's ideas happen. Let's have a party tomorrow!

YAY!

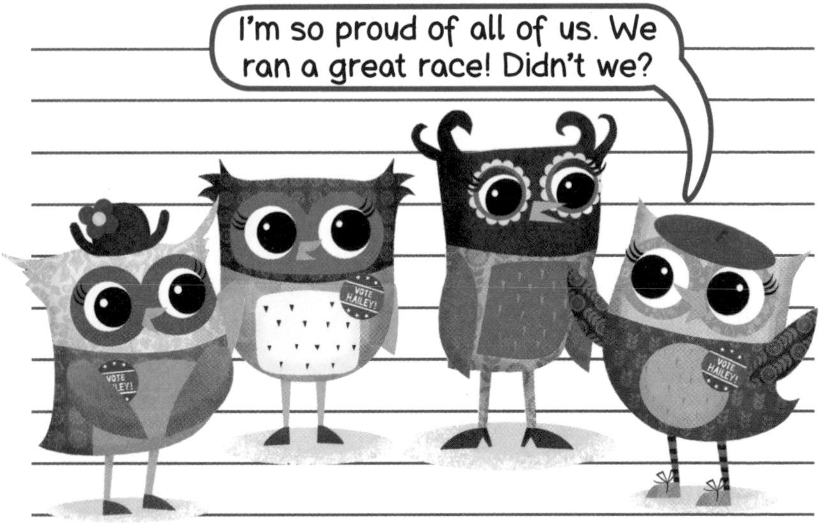
I'm so proud of all of us. We ran a great race! Didn't we?
VOTE HAILEY!

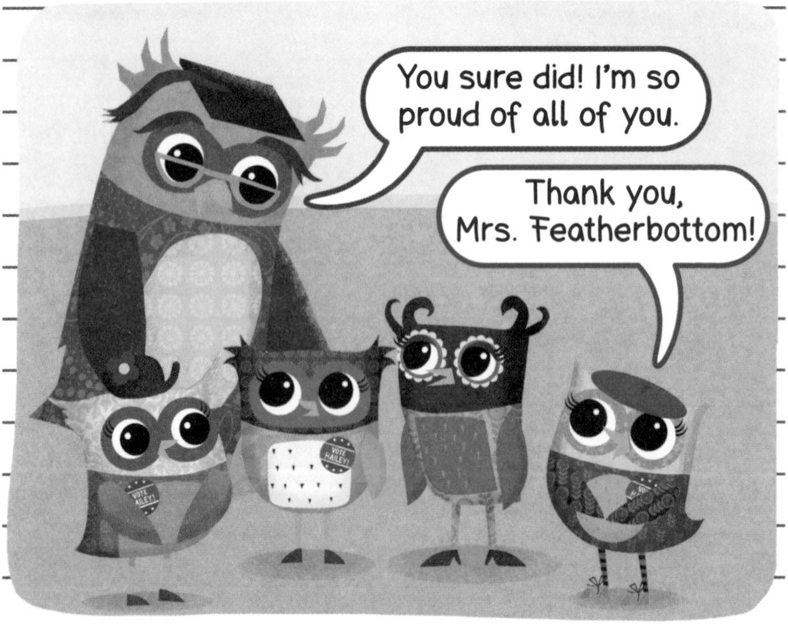
You sure did! I'm so proud of all of you.
Thank you, Mrs. Featherbottom!
VOTE HAILEY!

We are so lucky to have the best teacher!
You know, you're a lot like Mrs. F.
VOTE HAILEY!
VOTE HAILEY!
That's true, Eva!
You're great at helping owls do and be their best.
Oh wow, thank you!

What Sue, Hailey, and Lucy said to me really got me thinking. You know what, Diary? Maybe now I do know what I want to be when I grow up! You'll find out soon. Right now I need to get to sleep so I'm wide awake to party tomorrow!

7

♡ The President's Party ♡

Saturday

Tonight we all went to the Old Oak
Tree to have a party for our newly
elected class president, Hailey! This was
my party hat. What do you think, Diary?

Mrs. Featherbottom came along and my brother's band, the Hootles, played. It was **FLAPPY-FABULOUS** fun!

I can't wait to start making our school better!

Me too! We're going to make the best team!

PRESIDENT

VICE PRESIDENT

THE HOOTLES

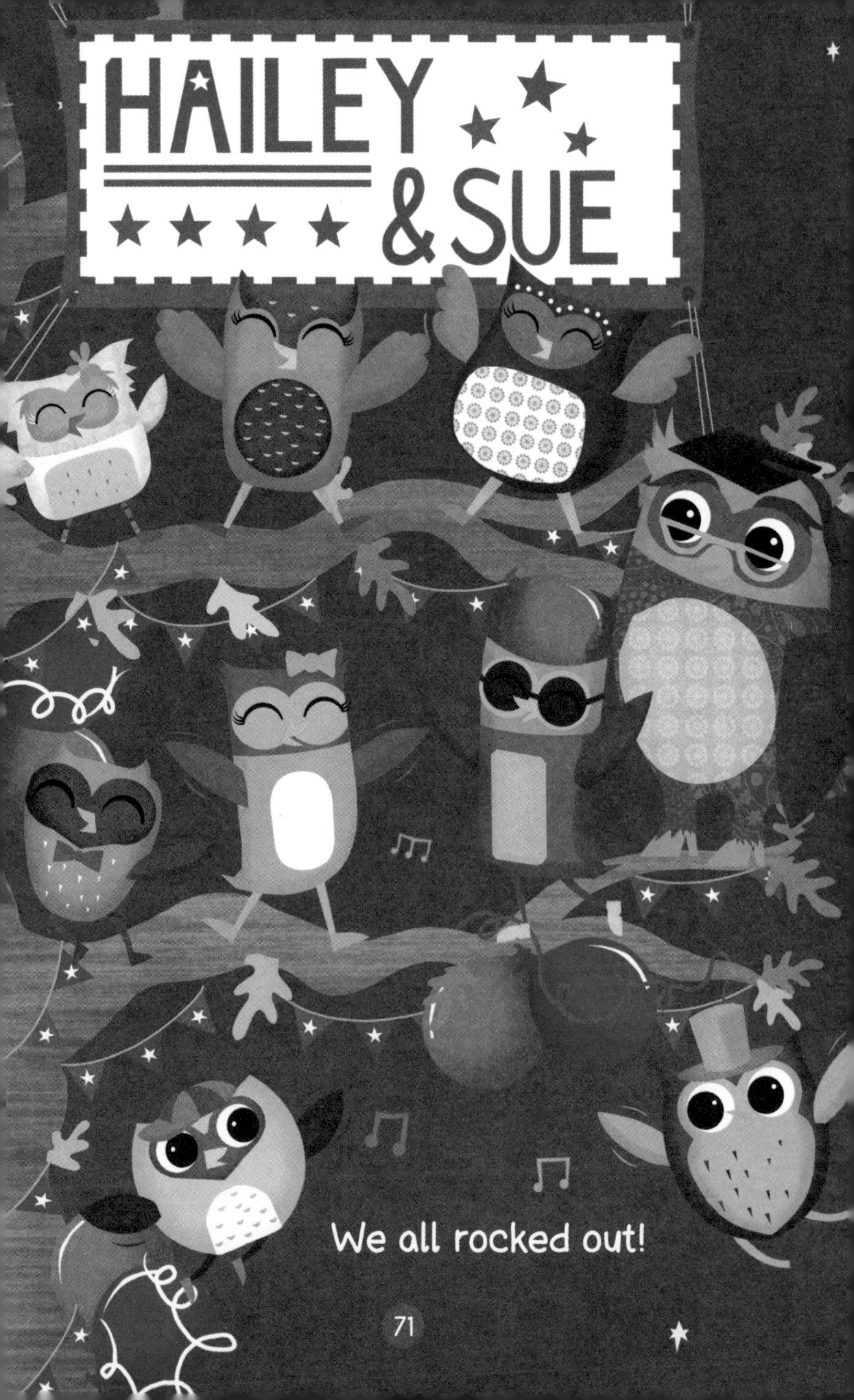
HAILEY
& SUE

We all rocked out!

Then I picked some flowers and gave them to Mrs. Featherbottom.

I wanted to thank you for everything you do for us all. Oh, and I think I know what I want to be — a teacher like you!

Oh, that's wonderful, Eva! You'll make the BEST teacher!

What an **OWLMAZING** Day! See you next time, Diary!

Rebecca Elliott was a lot like Eva when she was younger. She loved making things and hanging out with her best friends. Now that Rebecca is older, not much has changed — except that her best friends now include her two sons, Benjy and Toby. She still loves making things, like stories, cakes, music, and paintings. But as much as she and Eva have in common, Rebecca cannot fly or turn her head all the way around. No matter how hard she tries.

Rebecca is the author of several picture books, the young adult novel PRETTY FUNNY FOR A GIRL, and the bestselling UNICORN DIARIES and OWL DIARIES early chapter book series.

OWL DIARIES

How much do you know about Eva for President?

Mrs. Featherbottom asks all the students what they want to be when they grow up. Why doesn't Eva know how to answer this question at first? What does she decide in the end? And what do you want to be when you are older?

Sue is excited to run for class president. Why do none of the other owls want to run against her? What does Eva decide to do about it?

Reread chapter 3. Eva asks the class for suggestions on how to make their school better. What are some of the great ideas Eva, Hailey, and Lucy are given?

Reread pages 54 and 55. Why does Eva change her mind about running for president? What is the new plan Eva surprises Hailey and Lucy with?

Who does the class vote for as their class president? How do Sue and Hailey decide to work together?